Yo Gabba Gabba!™

EVERYONE IS DIFFERENT

adapted by Kara McMahon
based on the screenplay "Differences"
written by Scott Schultz

Simon Spotlight
New York London Toronto Sydney

HELLO, FRIENDS!

I want to tell you a story about the day my friend Muno got glasses. Muno needed the glasses to see better, so he was very excited when he got them. But then some of his friends said mean things because he looked a little different with his glasses on, and that hurt his feelings. Here's what happened:

I'm sorry, Toodee! I didn't mean to knock over your blocks. I didn't see them!

Maybe you need to get your eye checked!

So Muno went to see Plex and asked him to check out his eye.

And it turned out that Muno needed glasses!
These glasses will help you see where you're going, Muno!
Wow, thanks! Razzle-dazzle! I got glasses!

Muno was really excited! He couldn't wait to tell his friends. First he saw Foofa. She really liked his new glasses. She said nice things to him, and that made Muno feel good.

Then Muno saw Brobee and Toodee playing. They were surprised to see him looking a little different.

Muno, you look weird!

Yeah, Muno! You *do* look weird! Why do you look like that?

Muno's feelings were hurt. Brobee and Toodee didn't want to hurt Muno's feelings, but they accidentally said mean things. And then Muno wasn't sure if he still liked his glasses.

I don't want my friends to think I'm weird!

You look a little different in your glasses, but being different is fun!

Plex and Foofa tried to make Muno feel better.

Brobee and Toodee were just surprised because you look a little different. They don't really think *you're* weird!

Then Plex explained to Toodee and Brobee that they hurt Muno's feelings.

Muno is sad because you were mean to him. He might look a little different with his glasses on, but that's okay! They help him to see. You should never be mean. Saying Muno looks weird isn't nice.

I'm sorry, Muno! I didn't mean to be mean!
I'm sorry too! I like your new glasses! I was just surprised because you look a little different.

Muno was feeling a little better after his friends apologized. And then they sang him a wonderful song and he felt *much* better!

Your glasses make you look a little different.
But they help you to see and that's good!
We think you look GREAT in your glasses!
We love you; you're still you!
Being different is COOL!

Muno decided he really did love his glasses because they helped him to see. And he was happy that his friends liked them too!

We love your glasses too! And we love you!

Remember, friends, it's okay to be different! Being different is fun!

Muno is tall, and Brobee is short!

Foofa is pink, and Toodee is blue!

Muno has one eye, and I have two. But we both wear glasses!

Muno is bumpy, Brobee is furry, and Plex is smooth!

All of our friends are different, but we love them all the same!

My friend Brobee is small, but he has a great big heart, and I love him!

My friend Foofa has a flower on her head, and I love her!

My friend Toodee likes to ice-skate and I don't, but I love her!

My friend Gooble is always sad, but I love him!

All of my friends are different, and I love them all the same!

And now it's time to go! Thanks for listening to my story. Don't forget: Everyone is different. And being different is *great*!